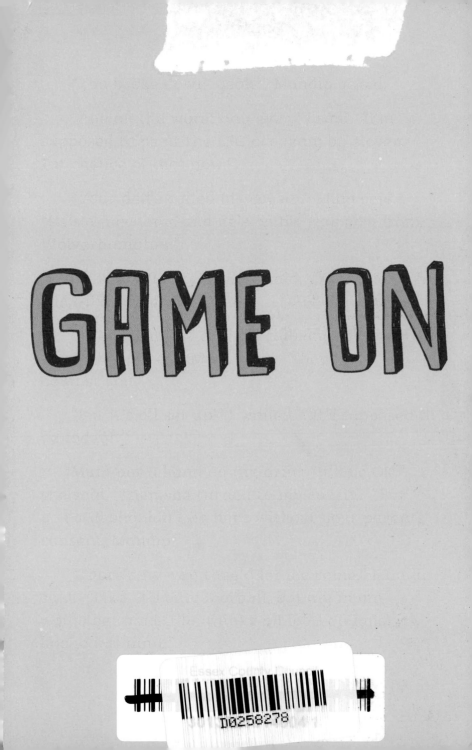

GAME ON

BALI RAI

GAME ON

Barrington Stoke

To the 96 who lost their lives at Hillsborough on April 15th 1989, and to their families.
And to everyone who fought for truth and justice, for so very long.

You'll Never Walk Alone.

First published in 2015 in Great Britain by
Barrington Stoke Ltd
18 Walker Street, Edinburgh, EH3 7LP

www.barringtonstoke.co.uk

Text © 2015 Bali Rai

A CIP catalogue record for this book is available from the British Library upon request

ISBN: 978-1-78112-448-2

Printed in China by Leo

CONTENTS

1. GONNA BE A STAR, INNIT!

"My son gonna be a footballer, innit?" my dad bragged.

I groaned. It was a Saturday night and I was working in my dad's chip shop. I should have been out with Hannah, my super-cute girlfriend. Instead I was stuck here, all hot and sweaty, and my dad was bragging to every single customer. Again.

"He gonna be a star, mate. Play for the England ..."

Dad put more chips into the fryer, as I turned to the next customer.

Lacey, who worked for my dad, was rolling up a portion of haddock and chips. "Are you that good?" she asked.

"I'm OK," I said. I felt a bit embarrassed.

See, a few weeks earlier, I'd been to a local football trial with my best mates Danny and Mo. And, after that, I'd been offered a second trial, this time with my favourite team. Liverpool FC. My local team, Leicester City, wanted me too. But all I cared about was Liverpool. It was like being hit by lightning.

LIVERPOOL FC.

I'd worshipped them since I was a kid and the fact I might get to play for them was all I could think of.

After I got the offer, I'd acted like a zombie clown, walking around with a permanent smile on my face and bumping into things. Every other word that came out my mouth was "huh" or "what?". It lasted until Hannah told me I was getting annoying.

Lacey handed over the fish to her customer. "Just imagine earning, like, a hundred grand a week," she said. "I'd be happy with a grand a week!"

"It's just another trial," I told her.

"Yeah right," she said, and grinned at me. "Get famous, Baljit. Then you can buy me a car. Maybe a big house, too."

"There's no guarantee I'll make it," I told her.

Only, inside, I didn't feel like that. I was going be a star player – that's what I told myself, every day. It was my dream.

★ ★ ★

Later, Hannah came into the shop. She had on a Bob Marley T-shirt, with purple jeans and purple Converse. Her hair was almost black and cut short. She grinned at me, and her honey-brown eyes sparkled.

"You look a bit hot," she told me.

"I am hot," I said. I wiped my brow. "There's people in the Amazon who ain't as hot as me. I need a shower."

Dad came out of the prep room behind the counter with a kebab order. We didn't do our kebabs in pitta bread. Ours were Indian-style – served on massive naan breads with yoghurt and chilli sauce. We sold proper curries too – Chicken Tikka Masala and Lamb Bhuna, and that. And in the counter, next to the battered sausages and fish cakes, we had samosas.

"Hello, Hannah!" Dad almost shouted. "You come to take my son away?"

Hannah smiled. "No, I was just passing by," she said.

"Rush is over – you go," Dad said. "Me and Lacey finish up, innit?"

I sighed with relief, went through to the back and took my apron off. I could smell the grease on my hair and clothes. Hannah followed me, and we went up to the flat above the shop.

"Sorry, it stinks a bit," I said, as we walked into the living room.

"Oh shut up!" Hannah said. "You say that every time I come round. I don't care."

"Yeah, but I do," I said.

"You do what?" I heard Mum ask from the door.

"Care that everything smells," I moaned.

"Moan, moan, moan," Mum said. "Why don't you cheer up? I thought it was your dream to be a footballer. How come you're so miserable?"

"Yeah, you grump," Hannah said, and she winked at my mum.

I was hot, sweaty and stank like a battered cod, and my girlfriend and my mum were picking on me. Some Saturday night this was.

"I'm going downstairs to help your dad," Mum said.

As soon as my mum left, Hannah jumped on me.

"Hello, smelly," she said, her mouth close to mine. "Fancy a snog?"

What a really, really stupid question. Saturday night had just got a whole lot better!

2. THE LIVERPOOL THING

It was nearly the end of term. My trial at LFC was two weeks away, and I was desperate for the wait to end.

Thing is, I also had a big game coming up for my league side – Field Rangers. We were neck and neck with our biggest rivals, Parkstone Majors, and our final game was at their ground. The winners would be league champions – and I wanted to finish the season with a medal.

Danny and Mo came round one night and we sat on a wall by the chip shop and talked tactics.

Danny was my oldest friend – he was more like a brother in fact. His birthday was the day after mine, and people called us twins, even though we didn't look anything like each other. I was average height and stocky, with Asian parents, and Danny was tall and wiry, with long legs. He looked a bit like Will Smith, the actor, and he was a joker. Or he thought he was, anyway.

"Gonna be a tough game," Mo said. "Parkstone Majors got some fast players up front, so we have to be careful. Defend tight."

Mo was Asian like me – only his parents were from Pakistan, and my dad's Indian. He'd lived in Oldham, near Manchester, and only moved to our school at the end of Year 7. He was a bit moody sometimes, but still a good laugh. For a Man United fan, that is.

"Look where being careful got you, Mo," Danny said. "No girl, no life and we're only your friends cos we feel sorry for your lonely ass!"

Mo swore at him and threw a joke punch, which Danny ducked.

"I'm serious," Mo said. "Parkstone Majors could do us some damage."

"They ain't that good," I said. "We've got much better players than them!"

"Yeah – proper quality. Don't get called to trials otherwise, would we ..."

Danny realised his mistake just as his sentence finished. "Shit, Mo," he apologised. "I didn't mean …"

See, me, Danny and Danny's cousin, Tyrell, were all offered interviews with top clubs after the local trials. Danny even got an invite to his favourites – Arsenal. But Mo got injured and didn't make it.

"It's OK, bro," Mo told him. "I know you didn't mean nothing."

"When's the next training session?" I asked.

"Tuesday, 7 p.m.," Danny said. "Then again on Thursday. Let's forget that for now, anyway – let's go up the High Street."

"Why?" Mo asked.

"Because I have a pretty-girl thirst," Danny joked. "And I need some water."

That was Danny all over – football, girls and PlayStation. I swear he never thought about anything else.

When I got in, Dad was closing up.

"Hardly any customers tonight," he said. "Bloody waste of time and electricity, innit?"

I smiled. Instead of saying "electricity", he'd actually said "electric city".

"What you smirking at?" he asked.

"Nothing, Dad," I said. "I'm just thinking about the Liverpool thing."

He yawned. "That still weeks away," he said.

"Two weeks," I told him. "We need to sort out the details. Like, who is coming with me and stuff."

Dad switched off the lights and I followed him upstairs.

"Your mum going," he said. "I got to open the shop. Her English better than mine, anyway. You just be embarrassed by me –"

"No I wouldn't!" I protested. "No way would I be ashamed of your accent. You're my dad."

He smiled and poured himself a big shot of whisky.

"You talk to your mum about the Liverpool," he told me. He leaned back on the sofa. "I'm tired."

Only Mum was making his dinner, so I went to my room. I didn't mind that my dad couldn't come with me. After all, I was lucky to be going at all. Until the letter came from Liverpool FC, my dad had never wanted me to be serious about football. He didn't see it as a proper career. In the end, I'd lied and pretended to be on a school trip so I could go to the trial. Only, when he found out, he didn't get angry. He just got used to it and started to support me. He might have a funny accent and mix up his words sometimes, but he was the best dad ever.

③. DANGER

A few days later, I was on the way home after football practice with Danny when we walked straight into danger. We were taking a short cut past a dodgy pub, when someone shouted racist abuse at us from the car park.

"Shit!" Danny said.

"What?"

I looked over and straight away I recognised the lad who'd abused us. He was a bit chunky with spiky blond hair and piggy eyes – and he went to our rival school.

"That's the lad from before," I said.

Danny clenched his fingers into fists. "Yeah, he's called Jordan," he said. "He's in with some older blokes – proper racist scum."

The lad smirked at us. His gang had chased us a few weeks ago, and then he'd turned up at the football trials – where the ref had sent him off for racism.

"Where's your red card now, Paki?" he shouted, as five of his mates got out of a knackered Ford Focus.

My legs were shaking and I wanted to run. I looked at Danny. "What we gonna do?" I asked.

The gang started to move towards us. Two of them were proper grown blokes.

"We can't take them all on," Danny said. "Head to the church and across the graveyard. We can lose them after the underpass."

The underpass would take us across the ring road, into "our" area. But it was a long way and the gang had a car. Only, what choice did we have? If we stood and fought, they'd batter us.

"Come on!" Danny shouted.

We ran for it. Danny was faster, but I didn't fall too far behind. I followed him across the road, and then we sprinted down a busy street full of shops and parked cars. People gave us funny looks as we weaved in between them, but I didn't care. I just wanted to get away.

About two minutes later, we reached the church, and I was gasping for breath. I turned my head and saw that the gang weren't behind us.

"Danny!" I shouted. "We lost them."

We stopped by the gate to the graveyard and Danny shook his head.

"They'll be in the car," he panted. "Trying to get around the other side of the ring road."

I hadn't thought of that. If they did that, they would cut us off. And then we'd really be in trouble.

"We need to keep going," Danny said. "Come on!"

We cut across the empty graveyard and along a path shaded by tall trees. A hundred metres away, a hedge shielded some metal railings. Beyond that was the ring road.

"Not far now," Danny shouted.

We were jogging now, getting closer to safety. All we had to do was jump the railings and we'd be at the underpass.

"Can't believe this racist shit," Danny said. "Them idiots need some education."

We climbed over the railings and were soon standing on the ring road. But it wasn't very busy, and we kept moving.

"You think we lost them?" I said as we walked down into the subway.

"Hard to know, bruv," Danny said. "They could be anywhere."

The subway walls were tagged with graffiti and it stank of damp. Someone had abandoned a buggy halfway down.

We took the stairs to the street. We couldn't see the gang anywhere.

"That was too close," I told Danny. "Next time, we'll go the long way home."

Danny flinched as a cracking sound echoed around us. Then a heavy thud. Someone was throwing bricks. There was a fenced-off building site to our left. I could see Jordan and his mates on the far side of the fence – swearing and shouting and finding things to throw.

"Effin hell!" I groaned as we set off again.

This time we didn't stop until we reached my dad's chippy. The place was empty and Lacey stood at the counter looking bored.

"You OK?" she asked. "You look like you've been running."

"Just messing about," I lied. I grabbed two cans of cola from the fridge. "Let's go upstairs," I said to Danny.

My parents were out, so we chilled in the living room, trying to calm down.

"They're gonna hurt somebody," Danny said. "We should report them."

"Who to?" I asked.

"I dunno," he said. "The police? Our parents?"

"Our parents would just ban us from going out and that," I told him.

"Yeah, but just imagine if they had caught us?" he said.

I shook my head. I didn't want to think about it.

"I'm telling you," Danny said. "Someone's gonna get hurt bad."

If we reported them, then we might stop Jordan and his thugs. But then I'd get grief off Dad. He'd want to know where I was all the time. Besides, I had more important things to think about. It was just over a week till my Liverpool trial.

"When's your Arsenal thing?" I asked Danny, to change the subject.

"Summer, sometime," he told me. "My mum is more excited than me, bruv!"

"She like crap teams too, then?" I joked.

"Leave it," Danny said. "We're gonna do you lot next season."

"Yeah, but not this one, eh?"

Liverpool had just finished higher in the league than Arsenal and I knew it wound Danny up.

"I'm going to Liverpool the weekend after next," I said. "I'm bricking it."

"I know," Danny said. "Some nights I get so wound up, I can't sleep." He grinned. "Like, what if we did make it, Baljit?"

"That would be awesome," I said. "Like, when we were kids and we used to pretend we were proper Premier League players on the park? It'll be like that but real."

"You know it," Danny said. "Once in a lifetime."

I imagined lifting the Champions League trophy for Liverpool. In my mind Danny was next to me, even though he was in an Arsenal shirt. We were both grinning like little kids.

4. CHOP, CHOP

Hannah came over after school on Friday. We watched some telly, and then I told her what had happened with Jordan.

"You should have called the police!" she said, shocked.

"What for?" I said. "They wouldn't have done anything. It would be our word against Jordan and his gang."

"Well – what about your dad?" Hannah sounded just like Danny.

"He'd go crazy," I told her. "He'd stop me going out and all sorts. Jordan and his gang are idiots. It's nothing serious."

Hannah gave me a weird look – like she thought I was crazy.

"They're racist thugs who threw bricks at you," she pointed out. "Is that nothing?"

"You know what I mean," I said.

"Not really," she said. "Why should you have to put up with abuse like that?"

"We shouldn't," I said. "But what can we do? We haven't got any evidence – Jordan would just get away with it."

Hannah started to say something but I stopped her.

"Forget him," I told her. "I've got to focus on the game tomorrow, and then Liverpool."

Hannah nodded, then looked away.

"What's up?" I asked.

"Nothing," she said, but I could tell she was lying.

"Hannah …?"

She stared into my eyes. She was so fit that every time I saw her, I wanted to kiss her. She even made our nasty school uniform look good. I felt myself blushing.

"When you're rich and famous," she said, "will you still remember me?"

I raised my eyebrows in surprise.

"You what?" I asked. "Why would I need to remember you? We're going out ..."

"Yeah, but when you're playing for Liverpool, earning all that money," she mumbled. "You'll be with a model or something – all those footballers are."

"I don't want a model," I told her. "I want you."

Hannah half smiled.

"So I'm not pretty enough to be a model, then?" she teased.

I felt like a complete tool. What a stupid thing to say.

"I don't mean you're not pretty," I said. "It's just that I thought you wanted to be a doctor."

"I do," she said, with a grin. "I just like winding you up."

"You're fitter than any model," I blurted out. "Like, much prettier – and much cleverer too!"

"Oh shut up!" she said. "Like I believe that. You're super weird sometimes."

"Ain't as weird as you," I told her.

Hannah grinned and punched my arm.

"Oww!"

"You're such a baby," Hannah said. "Anyway, what time have you got to help your dad?"

"In about an hour," I said.

Hannah walked over to my desk and picked up one of my PlayStation controllers.

"Just enough time to kick your bum at FIFA then," she said. "I'll be Man United."

Hannah wasn't even into football, but she was brilliant on the PlayStation. Much better than me.

"Now you're asking for it!" I said.

"Yeah, cos last time I beat you five–nil."

The shop was dead until just after 7 p.m. Then it went mad. By 9 p.m., I was tired, sweaty and grumpy.

"That was mad busy!" Lacey said. "I thought it'd never stop."

Dad grinned and shook his head.

"Busy shop mean more money, innit," he told her. "And more money mean more hours for you and more wages."

"You could just double my wages anyway," Lacey joked.

"I'll bloody double you in minute!" Dad said. Lacey and me burst into laughter. Like, what did that even mean?

I went into the stock room at the back of the shop and grabbed two cases of cola. Back in the shop, I was just getting into the second case when I heard him.

"Eh up, lads!" he said. "Look who I've found."

I turned to find Jordan staring at me. Behind him stood two teenage lads in jeans, trainers and puffa jackets.

"What do you want?" I said. I looked over at my dad. He was too busy with the customers to notice.

"This your shop, yeah?" Jordan asked.

I clenched and unclenched my fists as I nodded.

"Don't worry," he mocked. "I ain't stupid enough to kick off in here. You've probably got CCTV."

I nodded again. He was right. We had cameras inside and out, and they were always on, even when the shop was closed.

"Never mind," Jordan said. "I'll catch you on the street. Should be able to smell your curry breath coming."

I felt like smashing a can into his face. Only that would make me as bad as him.

"You got an order, love?" I heard Lacey ask.

Jordan turned.

"You talking to me, old lady?" he asked her. His tone was proper rude.

Lacey's smile disappeared.

"Do you have an order?" she asked again.

"Curry," one of Jordan's mates said. "Make it proper smelly, too."

My dad was busy chatting to someone, so he didn't hear.

"You want me to slap your spotty face off?" Lacey almost shouted.

This time Dad heard her.

"Lacey?" he said. "What happening?"

Jordan smirked at my dad's accent, and I almost forgot to stay calm. On his own, he was nothing – just a spotty, racist moron, swaggering in his green Adidas tracksuit.

"Nothing, Mr Sandhu," Lacey said. "Just little boys playing silly games. I've got it."

She walked to the counter flap and stepped out. I'd never seen her look so angry. Her eyes were blazing with rage. As she approached the lads, all of them started to back down, even Jordan.

"I ain't gonna ask again," she warned. "Now, do you wanna buy food or are you leaving?"

Jordan started to speak, but Lacey shushed him. She poked a finger into his chest and I wanted to laugh.

"Be careful, son," she told him. "I've taken on bigger men than you my whole life ... Beat every single one of 'em, too."

"Let's go," Jordan said to his mates. Then he turned to me and gave it the big one. "See you around, mate," he jeered.

"I hope so," I said. I wasn't going to back down. No way was he gonna think I was scared of him. No way.

"Thanks, Lacey," I said when they'd left. "You saved my skin there."

"No problem," she said. "Little turds like that need to learn about respect. Vile rats – they're from round my way. How do you know them?"

I didn't know how to explain, so I just said, "Football."

"Watch them," she said. "That Jordan Kent is a nasty piece of work, and so are his family. Horrible racists, the lot of them."

"He's a bully, that's all," I told her.

"Bully?" Lacey said. "He's a little git. He does anything, let me know. I'll kick his sorry ass, then fry him up and serve him with chips, smothered in curry sauce."

I believed her too.

"Everything OK?" Dad asked.

"All cool, Mr S," said Lacey. "Back to work – chop, chop – *jaldi jaldi!*"

I loved it when Lacey used an Indian word. Her accent was spot-on – she sounded just like my dad. I burst out laughing.

"You too, Baljit," she said. "Jump to it. You're not a famous footballer yet, kid!"

Just like Jordan and his mates, I did what Lacey said. She was proper scary.

5. TAKE IT EASY

Danny's dad drove me, Tyrell, Danny and Mo to Parkstone Majors for our match. Our coaches, Mamms and Winston, were already there, chatting to the other players and their parents. The Parkstone Majors team had arrived too, on the opposite side of the pitch.

"Big, big game," Mo said, like we didn't know that already. "We're gonna hammer them – believe dat!"

Tyrell went to talk to Mamms and Winston. I followed, but Danny pulled me to one side.

"We need to chat, bruv," he whispered. "Bout the game today. It's huge. But you and me have to think about the future."

I didn't have a clue what he was talking about.

"What if you get injured?" he said. "That's your future at LFC done, bruv."

I must have woken up stupid but at last I understood what Danny was on about.

"I didn't think about that," I admitted.

"I've been thinking about it all week, bro."

"So what do we do?" I asked.

"Take it easy," he said. "Play our game, but don't go in for no silly business, you get me?"

"But what about the team?"

"I feel wrong for saying it, but the trials are too important," Danny said. "The team will be here next year. You and me – we're going other places."

The team were one game away from being champions for the first time ever. We'd been awesome all season, winning games by record scores.

"I get what you're saying," I said, "but I don't want to let Mamms and Winston down."

"You won't," he insisted. "Just steer clear of any rough tackles and that. If you get hurt, you'll be proper gutted."

He was right. Imagine going up to Liverpool for an interview and being injured? All my dreams, all my hard work, would be wasted. Ruined.

Mamms and Winston called us together for warm-up drills, but I couldn't think of anything except Danny's warning.

"You awake, son?" Winston shouted at me. He was nearly two metres tall, with shoulders as broad as a door, and a shaved head. You didn't mess with him.

"Huh?" I said.

"Come on, Baljit!" he yelled. "Wake up – it's the big game!"

By kick-off, my team-mates were fired up – but I just kept looking at Danny. I couldn't help it. What he'd said had really got to me.

"You know we can do this!" Mo told us. "The league title is ours, lads!"

"You know the score," Winston said. "Same formation, same pressing and movement off the ball, same energy! This is what we've been working for all season. This is the big one!"

The rest of the team responded with cheers, but when I joined in, it was half-hearted. Mo shot me a sharp look.

"What's up with you?" he asked.

"Nothing," I said. "Just a bit nervous."

"Forget that!" he said. "No time for nerves, bro. We've got a game to win."

"I know," I replied.

Mo gave me a funny look and went off to take his position. Tyrell joined me. He played with me in central midfield, and he looked just as nervous as I did.

"Danny talk to you, too?" he asked.

I nodded.

"He's got a point," Tyrell said. "Last thing I want to do is mess up and get hurt."

I shook my head this time.

"Parkstone Majors ain't a dirty team," I told him. "They're good lads. If we play our best, we'll be fine."

★ ★ ★

The first half seemed to fly by. We did well, although I pulled out of at least three challenges. I also lost the ball a few times. At half-time it was 0–0, and Winston pulled me to one side.

"Where's your focus?" he said. "I've never seen you pull out of a tackle. What's up?"

"I'm OK," I said. "Just got a little knock on my ankle. Nothing major."

Winston looked down at my leg. "Do you want to come off?" he asked.

"No," I said. I felt awful for lying. "I'll do better next half, promise."

The coach nodded and went to chat to the others and Mo came over. He had nearly scored in the first half.

"You need to wake up," he said. "You and Tyrell are playing shit."

That was when I decided that I had to go for it. It was our last game and we needed to win it. I was letting my team down, and that wasn't fair on them. When Danny came over, I told him as much.

"Up to you," Danny said. "But use your brain, bruv. Think about your future."

My first touch in the second half nearly sent Danny clear on goal. The defender only tackled him at the last minute.

"Great pass!" Tyrell said.

"That's better!" Winston shouted from the touchline.

The game got faster, as both sides tried to take control. Parkstone Majors moved the ball fast. At times, I felt like I was chasing after shadows, but then, 15 minutes in, I broke into space between their midfield and defence. Mo gathered the ball and chipped it to me. I turned, skipped past one tackle, and ran at their defenders. Danny was on my right, and I knew he wanted a through-ball.

I slid the ball along the ground. Danny sprinted past his marker, and gathered it. He was through on goal, with just their goalkeeper to beat. A Parkstone Majors defender was closing him down, about to challenge, and I heard myself yelling "Shoooot!!!!!"

But Danny seemed to stumble. His left leg twisted and collapsed beneath him, and I heard a sound that I'll never forget.

CRRACK!

Danny screamed in pain and collapsed to the pitch. I felt my stomach knot up. Parkstone Majors' keeper shouted to the coaches, as he tried to make sure Danny was OK. And then he threw up. When I reached my friend, I saw what was wrong. Danny's left leg had snapped in two.

6. DREAM OVER

Winston tried to comfort Danny, and Mamms called for an ambulance.

The hospital was close and the paramedics arrived fast. They gave Danny some gas and put his leg in an air-cushion thing. Danny was crying and shaking in pain, and I felt sick.

"His studs must have got caught in the ground," one of the parents said.

"It was horrible," another mum said. "You could hear his bone crack. That poor lad ..."

Tyrell was sitting in the centre circle with some of the players, and I went over to him.

"Sorry," he said, "I couldn't look. Is Danny OK?"

I shook my head.

"They're taking him to hospital now," I said.

"I can't believe it," Tyrell said. "After everything he said about being careful. It's like a sick joke."

"I know," I said. "But people break their legs all the time. He'll be OK once it's fixed."

Thing is, I wanted that to be true but I wasn't sure. I had no idea if Danny would be OK. The break had looked horrific.

"What's happening with the game?" Mo asked.

"Who cares?" I said. "Stuff the game!"

"People get hurt," Mo said. "We still have to play."

"Not me," I told him. "Not after that."

Mo mumbled something I couldn't hear and turned away. I walked back towards the ambulance. Danny was on a stretcher, and they were lifting him into the back. The blue lights were flashing.

"How is he?" I asked Danny's dad.

"It's really bad, son," he said. His face was all twisted up with sadness.

"He'll be OK," Winston said, and he patted my shoulder. "They'll take care of him."

"I didn't even see how it happened," I said as the ambulance left. "Like, he was about to shoot and then ..."

"It was an accident," Winston said. "Just a stupid accident. No one's to blame."

"We were thinking about the trials," I admitted. "Me and Danny. He said he wanted to take it easy so he wouldn't get hurt."

"I didn't know that," Winston said.

"Do you think that's why he got hurt?" I asked. "Like, was it God or summat – what do you call it?"

"Tempting fate," the coach told me. "And, no, it weren't that. These things can happen. I broke my leg twice as a kid."

"But you still got to play, yeah?"

Winston nodded.

"So, Danny will be OK, won't he?" I said. "He'll still get to play for Arsenal and that ...?"

Winston didn't reply.

★ ★ ★

Twenty minutes later, the game was abandoned. Mo and some others started to complain when Winston told us. But me and Tyrell nodded. Neither of us wanted to play on, and I could tell Mo was unhappy with us.

"We'll rearrange the game," Winston said. "We'll let you know the new date at practice on Thursday night."

"Don't see why we can't play on today," Mo groaned.

"We just can't," Winston said. "It's not right, and the Parkstone Majors coach agrees with me. So does the ref."

"We should be thinking about Danny," I said. "Stuff the game. Danny's more important."

Most of the lads started to leave. But since Mr Dixon was at the hospital, Tyrell, Mo and me didn't have a lift.

"I'm going with Pally and his mum," Mo said, when I asked how he was getting back. Pally was our goalkeeper.

"I can take you two," Winston said. "If you like?"

"Cheers, coach," Tyrell said. He pulled his grey joggers over his shorts and changed his boots for trainers.

As I did the same, Mo walked off. He didn't even say goodbye. He was angry that his shot at glory for the season had been messed up and I was angry with him for wanting to play on. It was like he didn't care that Danny had been hurt. All he cared about was winning the game.

Winston's car was a ruby red Audi A4. It was awesome – black leather seats and a killer sound system. When he turned the key, the speakers burst into life, and a heavy bass line made the doors vibrate.

"Hope you like reggae?" Winston said. "Be a long walk home if you don't!"

I nodded but I wasn't thinking about the music, even though it was cool.

"You said you broke your leg twice?" I asked Winston, as we set off.

"Yeah," he said. He turned the volume down. "Twice in three years, when I was a teenager."

"Were you any good?" Tyrell asked from the back. "I mean, like did you play as a pro?"

"I did a couple of trials for City," Winston said. "But then, after I broke my leg, I wasn't the same."

"Why?" I asked.

"You start thinking about tackles." Winston shrugged. "At least I did. You pull back from your natural game, because you're always worried it might happen again. My leg wasn't as strong after it healed either."

I thought about Danny's love for Arsenal and I felt really bad for him. I was worried that it might be dream over for him.

"But I got my confidence back in the end," Winston added. "I've been playing football ever since."

"Yeah," I said, "but not at the same level."

"No," he said softly. "Not at the same level."

★ ★ ★

At home, I told my parents about Danny. They were really shaken. Later, I sat in my bedroom. I was feeling bad. Like, angry and sad at the same time. Guilty, too. What if I made it as a pro footballer and Danny didn't? What if Danny got angry with me, like Mo was, or stopped being my friend? All these thoughts were spinning around my head. I was proper mixed-up. I thought about texting Hannah, but I didn't. I thought about calling Danny's mum, but that didn't happen either.

In the end, I stretched out on my bed and shut my eyes. Only I couldn't sleep. All I could hear was the sound of Danny's leg breaking.

It wasn't fair. Why did Danny have to get hurt, and why now? And what was I supposed to say when I saw him? We'd dreamed of being footballers since we were little kids. Now it felt like my best friend's dream had died, and I didn't know how he would cope. Especially if I made it at Liverpool FC.

7. FEELING GUILTY

The next week was difficult. I should have been excited about going to Liverpool, but I wasn't. All I could think about was Danny. And I fell out with Mo at school on the Monday.

"You were proper selfish on Saturday," he said, as we sat at lunch.

I pushed my pasta around on the plate.

"Selfish how?" I asked.

"You weren't bothered at all," he said. "All you care about is your LFC trial. You don't care about the team."

"I do care," I told him. "But winning the league isn't important when Danny got hurt like that."

Mo pulled a face.

"You were taking it easy before Danny broke his leg," he said. "That was just a freak accident."

"No I wasn't," I protested, but it was a lie. I had been taking it easy, and I felt twisted up with guilt about it.

"You, Danny, Tyrell – you think you're better than the rest of us," Mo said. "The other lads agree with me."

"Which other lads?" I snapped, angry now.

"Pally and them," Mo snapped back.

"Oh – so you're best mates with Pally now?" I said.

"He's a better mate than you," Mo said. "At least he cares about the team."

"And you care about Danny, do you?" I snarled. "He was screaming in pain and you wanted to play on. Even the other team wanted to postpone the game!"

Mo shrugged. "People get hurt," he said. "Like that Chelsea player who broke his ankle? They didn't stop the game, did they?"

"That's different," I told him. "We're not pros. You can't even compare the two things. It's stupid!"

Mo's face went red and he pushed his plate away.

"No!" he shouted. "You know what is stupid? Stopping a game just because someone got hurt. It's no big deal. Danny will be playing again by the start of next season."

"But he'll miss his trial!" I said.

"So what?" Mo snapped. "Who says he's gonna make it anyway?"

That made me see red. I wanted to hit him but I didn't. Mo was my mate, even if he was acting like a knob. Instead, I got up and walked away.

I was still annoyed the next day, when Hannah asked me over. She lived in a big, detached house in a posh area. My dad wanted to move into the same neighbourhood, and had started looking for somewhere. I'd be glad not to live over the chippy any more. We sat in Hannah's garden, as her mum mowed the lawn.

"Have you spoken to Danny?" Hannah asked. She was wearing faded shorts and an old T-shirt, but she still looked gorgeous. If I'm honest, I couldn't stop glancing at her legs.

"I sent him a couple of texts," I said. "I'm gonna go and see him tomorrow, after school."

"I can't even imagine how much it must have hurt," Hannah said. "Horrible." She pulled a face and shuddered.

"I can't imagine how Danny got hurt so bad," I told her. "And now he'll miss his trial at Arsenal. Like, what if I make it and he doesn't?"

"You can't think like that," Hannah said. "If you make it, Danny will be well happy. He's your best friend. What happened wasn't your fault!"

"But he might be angry," I said. "Because he's the one who got hurt, and I'm OK."

"Look," she said, "focus on yourself. The trial is this weekend, isn't it?"

"Yeah," I said.

"So, go and see Danny, and then start thinking about the trial – it's your big chance."

Hannah's words made sense, but her voice sounded sad.

"What's up?" I asked.

"Nothing."

"You seem a bit upset, that's all," I said.

"It's nothing," she repeated. "I was just thinking about you going away. To Liverpool."

We spent the rest of the afternoon chatting, and then I had dinner with her family. When I was about to leave, Hannah gave me a kiss, and then a big hug

"You OK?" I asked.

"Yeah," she said. "I really like you."

"I really like you too," I told her. "Are you sure you're OK?"

"Yeah," she said again. "Really. Just stop thinking about me and Danny and focus on your football."

I didn't ask her what she meant at the time. It was only later that I thought about what she'd said. Why did I have to stop thinking about her or Danny, just because of football?

★ ★ ★

Danny smiled when I walked into his living room the next day.

"Yes bruv!" he said.

He looked OK, considering. He was on the sofa, his left leg in plaster. He'd been playing FIFA on his Xbox, and the controller was on his lap. The area around him was littered with sweet wrappers and cans of Diet Coke.

"Easy life!" he joked. "I get to sit here and play my games and music, and Dad don't say a thing. It's like being a prince or summat, bro. I just click my fingers and I get what I like. Had KFC yesterday, Burger King the day before. Mum's getting me Nando's tonight!"

It sounded great, but I wasn't sure it was worth having a broken leg for.

"How you feeling?" I asked.

"Better," he said. "But I have to take major painkillers."

"Is your leg fixed?"

Danny shook his head. "This plaster is temporary – they're gonna operate on Friday. They're gonna pin my bones together. I'll be like some super hero, bruv. Like Iron Man or summat!"

I took a sip of my drink. "Is it that bad, then?" I asked.

"Yeah."

"Danny, I'm really sorry. I –"

He cut me off. "It's OK," he said. "It weren't your fault."

"I know that," I said. "But I feel bad. It's not fair, bro."

On the way over, I'd decided not to say anything about football or the trials, but maybe Danny wanted to talk about them. I thought he'd be too upset, but he seemed fine.

"But you'll be able to play, won't you?" I said. "Like, when it's fixed?"

"My leg broke in two places," Danny said, "and the ligament damage is really bad. That means another operation. I don't think I'll be the same again."

"You don't know that," I said. "Not for sure."

"Come on, Baljit," he said. "I'm a bit dim, bruv, but I ain't that stupid. The doctor reckons the leg won't be ready to walk on for about two months, and that's if I'm really, really lucky. She told me my knee damage was some of the worst she'd ever seen."

"But what happened?" I asked, beginning to feel really bad.

"I dunno," Danny admitted. "Like, I had the ball under control, and I was gonna place it to the keeper's left, and then the next thing ..."

He didn't finish. Instead, he looked away, and I asked the stupidest question ever.

"Did it hurt?"

Danny grinned at me. "Bruv!" he said. "What do you think? It was like the worst pain ever!"

"Yeah, you were screaming and crying on the pitch," I told him, "but it's no big deal. No one laughed at you or nothing. I would have battered anyone that did."

"I don't remember nothing but the pain, and when they gave me that gas, I was out of it," Danny said. "Then I woke up with this plaster on."

"The game got abandoned," I told him.

Danny nodded. "Yeah, Dad said. When's it rearranged for?"

"Mamms and Winston are gonna let us know at Thursday practice."

"Reckon you'll lose without my skills!" Danny said with a grin.

"I fell out with Mo, too," I added.

"Huh?" The grin left his face fast. "Why?"

I sat back and took another sip of my drink. Then I told my best friend everything.

8. A BAD OMEN

The morning of my trip to Liverpool, I was up really early.

Outside, the sun was bright and the birds were singing. I should have been happy and excited, but I wasn't. My thoughts were all over the place. My insides felt like they'd been twisted into huge knots, and I struggled to swallow the orange juice I poured myself.

At 6.30 a.m., Mum came in and asked what I was doing.

"Couldn't sleep," I told her. "Too nervous."

Mum sat down next to me. Her long black hair was messy and she looked tired.

"Your grandfather always said that life is about taking chances," she told me.

"Your dad?" I asked.

She nodded. "He taught me that everyone should dream. And if you go for your dreams, sometimes they come true. But sometimes they don't ..."

"I'm scared that my dream won't come true," I admitted.

"There's no need to be scared," she said. "You can only do your best. And if that isn't enough, you accept it and find another dream."

"But what if you want something so bad, that failing at it makes you sad?" I asked.

Mum smiled and put her hand on mine. "You get over it and move on," she said. "Or you try again. Either way, you never give up. There's a future out there for you, Baljit, and when it comes, you'll know what to do."

And with that, Mum went off to make breakfast.

★ ★ ★

We were on the motorway by 8 a.m. As we headed up the M1, I was jangling with nerves.

"Mum, the speed limit is 70 miles per hour," I said. "Not 45."

"No need to rush," she told me. "We left in plenty of time, and we'll be there in plenty of time."

"But what if there's traffic later on?"

"Let me do the driving," she said. "You focus on your trial."

From the M1 we took the A50 and from there we'd join the M6 North. The journey was taking for ever and I watched the world go by, bored. As we passed Stoke City's Britannia Stadium, I got desperate for a pee.

"We'll stop at the next service station," Mum said.

"But will we be late if we stop?" I asked.

"Stop worrying, Baljit."

The Sat-Nav fixed to the windscreen said we'd arrive at Liverpool's Academy by 9.53. Our meeting was at 11, so we had time. The motorway was clear, and soon Mum had pulled up at Sandbach services.

As she parked, a coach-load of Man United fans arrived. Talk about a bad omen. Only I couldn't understand why they were going to Old Trafford. The season was over, so it couldn't be for a game. When a second coach arrived, I grew even more confused.

Inside, as I waited for the toilets, I realised that every single Man United fan had a Brummie accent. Just my luck!

When I was done, I went out to the front to wait for Mum. The United fans were busy buying breakfast and coffee, and chatting about the testimonial game they were going to. The game was against Everton. Liverpool's two biggest rivals were playing each other – thank God I wasn't wearing my LFC shirt!

When Mum joined me, she gave them a wary look.

"Come on," she said. "Let's get away from these people."

"Don't be silly, Mum," I said. "They're just going to a game."

"I've seen the news," Mum said. "Rioting and drinking and shouting. Let's go."

Outside, as we walked past the coaches on the way to Mum's car, I thought I heard a familiar voice. It sounded like my Brummie cousin, Mandip, but it couldn't have been her. She wasn't into football, and no way was she a Man United fan.

We got in the car and Mum put her key in the ignition. I waited for the engine to growl into life. Nothing happened. The car shuddered, lurched forward, then stopped.

"Mum?"

"I must have stalled it," Mum said. "One minute."

She tried again, and this time the engine made a loud "PUT-PUT-PUT" sound.

"Mum!" I said again. I was getting paranoid now.

"Calm down, Baljit," she said. "It's just playing up."

But after three more attempts to start the engine, Mum gave up.

"I think we've broken down," she said. Her face was serious.

"No way!" I shouted. "Try again!"

Mum turned the key again.

The engine was completely dead. All I could hear was a ticking sound.

"Call the AA," I told her. "They'll fix it, won't they?"

Mum got out and I followed. She called my dad on her mobile. She turned away and spoke in a quiet voice, and I wondered what she was doing. Why call my dad and not the AA?

Behind me, some United fans were standing by their coach in their bright red shirts. They were mostly Asian, and some of them even wore turbans. It was like a Punjabi day out.

"Gonna be awesome, innit!" said that familiar Brummie voice.

"Mandip?" I said. "What you doing here?"

My cousin went as red as her United shirt. My mum looked at Mandip, and then at the stacks of male United fans with her.

"Mandip?" Mum said, raising an eyebrow.

"Hey." Mandip looked sheepish. "Fancy seeing you two here."

9. SMALL WORLD

After an awkward moment, Mandip decided to stop being sheepish. She walked over and hugged my mum.

"I'm going to a game," she explained. "My friend Kam is a huge United fan and I've been going with her for about six months."

"You never told me that!" I said.

"You're an LFC fan," she pointed out. "Like you want to hear about my new love for Man United."

Mum eyed the other supporters with suspicion.

"This Kam," she asked, "is she with you today?"

My family have always been fairly traditional when it comes to my female cousins. They expect them to stay home and be "honourable".

My mum was quite British in her attitudes, but she was still worried to see Mandip with so many blokes, and without her family.

"She's in the loo," Mandip told us. "Those guys over there are her family. And her brother runs the supporters' club."

"Do your parents know you're here?" Mum asked.

Mandip looked away, and I knew that she'd been caught out.

"Mum!" I said. "Forget Mandip. What about the AA?"

Mum shook her head.

"Your dad cancelled the membership because it cost too much," she said. "The car's only worth a few hundred quid."

'Typical tightwad Dad,' I thought. He was always on about saving money. But it was the only car we had. And now I was stuffed and so was he. How would he buy supplies for the chippy with no transport? How would I get to Liverpool? Talk about a stupid thing to do!

"You broke down, yeah?" Mandip asked.

"And on the worst day ever," I said. "I'm supposed to be at the LFC academy by eleven. Fat chance of that now."

"Your dad's called his cousin," Mum said. "He's a mechanic and he's on his way now from Wolverhampton."

"But that'll take ages!" I said. "And what if he can't fix the car?"

"Then we'll just call the club and tell them what's happened," Mum said. "They won't hold it against you."

"But it's all set up!" I wailed. "It's supposed to be today!"

Mum put a hand on my arm. "It'll be OK," she said. Then she turned to my cousin. "But you still shouldn't be here without your parents' consent, Mandip."

"There's no way they'd let me come," Mandip said. "Like, it's only football, but my mum would get mad. She thinks all football fans are hooligans, innit."

I could feel my LFC dream dying, but I still smiled at that. Mandip sounded just like me when I'd lied to my parents to go to the first football trials.

"Your mum's right, Mandip," Mum said. "Football fans are always fighting."

"Only the idiots," Mandip told her. "Most of us are just normal people."

She pointed to a huge man in a navy turban, whose beard grew down onto his chest. He wore a United home shirt, and when he turned away from us I saw "Bains" printed on the back. Bains was my mum's name before she married my dad.

"That's Kam's uncle," Mandip said. "He runs the local Sikh temple. Is he a hooligan?"

An older white bloke who was standing by the coach waved at her.

"And that's Mr Hurst," she added. "He's my history teacher. See? We're all normal. No big deal."

"Then why not tell your parents?" Mum asked. "Why lie to them, Mandip?"

"Look," I nearly shouted in frustration. "Can we just forget about Mandip and think about how I'm gonna get to Liverpool?"

"No need to shout," Mum said, as my cousin's mate Kam joined us. "We'll think of something."

"Hello!" Kam said. She looked from me to Mum. "Is something up?"

Her accent was milder than Mandip's and she had a really friendly face, with pale brown eyes and a beaming smile.

"This is my aunt," Mandip told Kam. "And this is my cousin, Baljit. He's the one I told you about."

Kam's face lit up. "You the footballer?" she asked.

"Sort of …" I said. "I'm meant to be at an interview at LFC's academy."

"Only they broke down, so he's stuck," Mandip said.

Kam told us to wait a moment. She went to speak to her uncle, the big Sikh guy by the coach.

She pointed over at us, then the two of them came over.

"My niece says you're in trouble?" Kam's uncle asked, as my mum squinted at him.

"So you're a Bains?" Mum asked him. She'd seen the back of his shirt too.

The man nodded. "Jag," he said, holding out his hand, "but everyone calls me Jacko."

Mum did the squint thing again. "I know your father," she said.

And with that, the two of them started their own conversation, and Mandip pulled me to one side.

"You've gotta help me," she said. "Mum can't find out I'm here!"

"Too late," I told her. "My mum is deffo gonna tell your mum. Not a lot I can do about that."

"My parents are gonna do their nut, innit," Mandip said.

She looked close to tears and I thought hard about how I could help her. Only I couldn't even help myself. Time was ticking by and I still had to get to Liverpool.

But then Kam's uncle snapped me out of my thoughts.

"Well," he said, with a smile, "it's a small world. Turns out we're related."

Then Mum went into this long-winded explanation of how she was connected to Kam's uncle. If we weren't stuck, it would have been funny. It's not so much that the world is small, but that my family is huge. If you add up all our distant relatives, it's like a football crowd. And there's no Punjabi word for cousin, which means that everyone in your generation is like a brother or sister. And I mean *everyone*.

"Anyway," Jacko said when Mum had finished. "We'll drop you off."

"Huh?" I said. I'd not been expecting that.

"We'll drop you off," Jacko repeated. "On the coach. It's only thirty miles out of the way and we're very early for the game."

"You're going to drop me off at LFC's academy," I said. "In a Man United Supporters coach?"

"Yeah." Jacko grinned. "No big deal. Happy to help out family – even Liverpool fans, eh?"

I thought about all the stories I'd heard about how much Man United and LFC fans hated each other. Yet, here I was, about to lose out on my big LFC dream, and some United supporters were coming to my rescue. Talk about weird.

"Come on then," Jacko said. "No time to lose."

I felt bad for Mandip that her secret was out. But I was also excited again. I was setting off for my interview – in a coach full of United-mad Brummies!

10. THIS IS ANFIELD

When we arrived at the LFC academy, a few people were hanging around the doors. As the coach pulled up, they gave us odd looks. As me and Mum got off, the looks got even odder.

"You lost, lad?" one bloke asked.

"Wrong end of the M62, son," another one said, with a grin. "Manchester's the other way!"

Mandip got off the coach and gave me a hug.

"Good luck," she whispered. "And please talk to your mum. If my parents find out, I'm in big trouble."

I promised her I would try. As the coach set off, I followed Mum inside. It was nearly eleven and I was just happy to be there.

"Relax. We're here now," Mum said, as a man in a red LFC tracksuit and black shorts came out.

"Mrs Sandhu?" he asked in a Scouse accent. "I'm Phil – and this must be Baljit."

He gave me a big grin. "I've been expecting you," he said. "Journey OK?"

Mum shook her head. "We broke down on the M6," she told him.

"But some nice people gave us a lift," I added. I wondered if I should mention they were Man United fans.

"Great!" he said. "Now, let's crack on. If you'd like to follow me ..."

He led us down a corridor, past a load of offices. At the end, he ushered us into a room, and we sat down again.

I looked around. There was a desk, with a Mac on it, and piles of folders. A whiteboard was fixed to one wall, and the others had posters stuck to them and one of those famous "This Is Anfield" signs.

"That's to remind the lads what they're playing for," Phil said, with a nod at the wall. Then he picked up a file.

"This is the first stage," he told my mum. "We're tight for time, so would it be OK to start?"

Mum nodded and he went on. "Our academy is one the best in Europe. It's a state-of-the-art facility over 56 acres, and is dedicated to youth development."

"It's very nice," I blurted out. Talk about stupid.

"Yes," said Phil, "it is. Anyway – there are two things we need to do today. First, Baljit, you're going to meet Scott. He does performance analysis. He'll take notes on your trial session. We've organised a mini-game with some of our lads and you'll take part. Is that OK?"

I nodded and gulped down air. I felt my stomach churn with nerves. I was going to be up against some of the best young players in England.

"Meanwhile, I'll chat to your mum about the boring stuff," Phil said. "If we decide to offer you a place here, and you decide to take it, there are decisions to make. Those decisions need your parents' full consent."

I nodded again, even though I had no idea what he was talking about. What decisions?

"Right," he said. "Let's get you over to Scott."

I grabbed my bag and followed Phil down another corridor, into a big hall with a low roof. A young coach smiled at me. He had a thick beard and was wearing the same as Phil – a red LFC training top and black shorts. A real football pitch with half-size goals at each end took up most of the space in the hall.

"Hi, Baljit," the coach said. He held out his hand and we shook. "I'm Scott. I'm one of the coaches who scouted you. Welcome to our academy."

"I'll see you later on," Phil told me. "Relax and enjoy the game."

"I'll try," I said, even though I still felt a bit sick.

"Ninety per cent of lads don't do well because they're nervous," Phil added. "Take it steady and think clearly – and you'll be fine."

As Phil left us, Scott looked at my bag.

"Do you have indoor football trainers?" he asked.

"Yes," I said. "I've got some outdoor boots and kit too."

"The trainers are all you'll need," Scott said. "We'll give you an LFC training kit to take home."

"Really?"

"Yep – now let's crack on."

Ten minutes later I was doing drills. Scott placed some cones around a circuit, and asked me to warm up. After 15 minutes of jogging and sprinting, he told me to stretch my legs. Then he handed me a size 4 football.

"TABS," he said.

"Huh?"

"It's what we look for," he explained. "Technique. Attitude. Balance. Speed. It's why I wanted to take another look at you after the trials in Leicester."

He pointed at the wall behind me, and I saw a banner with all four words on it.

"I want you to run with the ball at your feet," he said. "Keep your head up and try not to look at the ball."

I nodded – I knew the drill from Winston and Mamms' training sessions. Only those were held on our local park. This was completely different.

"Work around the cones, and once you're happy, pick up the speed. OK?"

I nodded.

"Go!"

I started badly. The ball just wouldn't go where I wanted, and I felt like an idiot.

"Stop thinking too much," Scott shouted. "Just do what's natural. I've seen you run with the ball in a real game. Head up!"

I took some deep breaths. Then I started again. This time I killed it. When I was done, Scott was beaming.

"Excellent!" he said. "Let's move on."

We went over to the far end of the hall, where nine lads had gathered by the goal.

"These are some of the under-15s – all around your age or a bit older," Scott said.

Five of the lads had yellow training bibs on. The other four wore green ones. They seemed really chilled, even though they were official LFC students. I wondered how I'd feel in their place.

"We're going to play 5-a-side," Scott told me. "Like Futsal – you know?"

I nodded. I loved Futsal. Scott asked me to join the lads in green. I picked up my bib and put it on. My new kit felt great and when I looked at the LFC club badge, I felt a surge of pride. But would I be good enough against these players? They were like the best of the best.

The game was much faster than anything I'd played in before. And the other lads were awesome. I struggled to get near them. They were way too good. I started to get annoyed with myself. My team was losing 6–3 too. Scott pulled me to one side at half-time.

"I was rubbish!" I told him, too frustrated to hide my feelings.

"These lads have more experience than you," Scott replied. "Their skill levels are very high."

He pointed at a lad called Jacob. "He's 14," Scott said, "and he plays for England under-16s already."

"So how am I supposed to compete with them?" I asked, still upset at being so outclassed.

"It's not about competing," Scott said. "Today is about seeing how you react and perform. Remember – TABS."

I made an effort to pull myself together. My confidence grew and I felt stronger in the second half. I got involved more, and then, with the score at 8–6 to the yellows, I played an assist for a goal.

"GOOD LAD!" Scott shouted. "Great pass – excellent!"

The game ended 9–8 to the yellows, but I felt much better. Some of the lads shook my hand and congratulated me. It was the best feeling. I felt like I belonged.

"Right," Scott said. "Time to warm down, Baljit."

"Is that it?" I asked, trying not to sound like a spoilt child.

"For today," Scott said with a grin. "We've got another lad due in an hour. Someone just like you. From Birmingham ... You did great, Baljit," he added. "You really held your own in the second half. Well done."

Half an hour later, I rejoined my mum and Phil. Mum had a load of folders and leaflets in front of her, and another cup of tea.

"How did that go, Baljit?" Phil asked, even though I knew he'd spoken to Scott about my session.

"OK, I guess," I said. I could play it cool now I'd calmed down a bit.

"Great," he said. "Your mum and I have spoken about the details and she's had a tour.

But there are things to work out. As an academy, we have to follow specific rules ..."

I wondered what he was on about.

"In order to take up your place, you'll need to move to the local area," he said.

"Move?" I said.

I hadn't even considered that I'd have to move. But how else could I play for Liverpool? But the thing was, how could I move to a new city and leave everything behind. What about my parents? What about Hannah and Danny?

"Your mum and I have discussed it," Phil said. "All that remains is for you to make up your mind."

His voice sounded like a distant echo in my ears. Only the last bit stood out. Make up my mind? Did that mean ...?

"I'm going to discuss things with my boss but I'm hoping to offer you a place here for two years, Baljit. If you accept, you'd start by September, so your schooling isn't disrupted. We don't need an answer now, but ..."

I swallowed hard and my legs started to shake. They were offering me a place. It was like being part of the best dream ever.

"Thanks for coming along today," Phil said. He stood and we shook hands. "Well done, lad."

I might have thanked him, but I can't be sure. I was too busy dreaming.

11. PROBLEMS

My head was spinning for a whole week after I got back. LFC was the only thing on my mind. I couldn't sleep, and when I ate, I couldn't taste my food. I was excited and nervous and scared all at the same time. Everyone seemed dead pleased for me, even Mo, who'd made up with me by then.

So when Hannah got angry with me, the next Saturday evening, I was shocked.

We were ordering chicken in Nando's, when she snapped.

"You're not even listening!" she shouted.

"Huh?"

"What did I just say?" she asked.

I tried to remember but I couldn't. It's hard to remember something you didn't hear in the first place, and I felt really bad.

"Er ..." I said, which was beyond stupid.

"See?" she snapped again. "All you care about is football!"

"No I don't," I protested. "It's just a big thing, that's all."

Hannah seemed to calm down, but later, when we got to her house, she just went indoors. No kiss, no nothing. As I walked home, I wondered why she was so upset. I couldn't work it out.

And when I visited Danny the following afternoon, he was acting just as weird.

"Are you sure you're OK with this?" I asked him.

When he looked away, I knew that he wasn't.

"It's hard," he began. "Like, every time you talk about the LFC offer, I think about my leg."

I nodded because I understood. I would have been the same.

"And if you leave," Danny added, "it's like I've lost my best mate and my big chance to play pro."

"But I'm not gonna stop being your friend," I insisted. "I'll be back loads."

"Ain't the same though, is it?" Danny said. "You know – like chatting at school and chilling out after football practice – all them things will go."

"We'll text and that," I said.

"Still not the same," he told me.

I knew he was right.

That evening, my parents joined in too. Dad was watching telly when I got in. He looked at me and nodded.

"Come and sit down," he said. "We must discuss this Liverpool thing."

I wondered what he was about to say as I joined him on the sofa.

"You know we very proud of you?" he asked.

I nodded, embarrassed.

"But this moving to Liverpool," he went on. "It bothering me … Not saying don't go, innit. But moving not easy for your mum and me."

"The club put players up with families," I told him. "They have these house parents who look after lads from other cities –"

"But I don't want to losing you to someone else," Dad said. "I want to be with my boy. You're my son, Baljit."

He looked so sad and I felt awful. In my head, I was already at LFC. I hadn't thought about my parents and how they would feel.

"I don't want to upset you, son," Dad said. "That would be unfair, innit. But if I not telling you how I feel, that unfair too. Your mum and me –"

"What does Mum think?" I asked.

"She happy for you, but she upset too," Dad said. "I can't lie to you, boy. She thinking we gonna lose you."

"But imagine if I make it," I said. "You and Mum can retire. No more long hours and smelly fish and chips."

Dad gave me a little smile. "I liking long hours," he told me. "It my work, innit? Everything we got, we getting because of smelly fish and chips."

"Like the new house you want to buy?" I asked.

Dad nodded. "No point in that now, son," he said. "If you going, what we need bloody big house for?"

I was their only child and that mattered. Punjabi people lived for their families. It wound me up sometimes, but I understood it. Especially for my mum and dad, who had wanted more kids after me, but couldn't.

"I'm sorry, I don't wanting you feel guilty," Dad said.

"It's OK," I told him. "You're just being honest. But this is a big chance for me, Dad. Like, this is the dream ..."

"Then you ignoring what this silly old man saying," he replied. "Then you go for your dream."

After dinner I went for a walk to clear my head, to think. Hannah, Danny, my parents – they were all upset at the thought of me leaving. As I walked down the High Street, I wondered if that was why Hannah had snapped at me. If I left, we wouldn't see each other very much. What if she dumped me because I was never around?

I had all these things to think about. Should I go to Liverpool? Should I stay? What should I do about Hannah and Danny? How should I deal with my parents' feelings?

I was so caught up in my own thoughts that I didn't see them coming.

"Oi! Taliban!"

My blood froze. I turned round to see Jordan Kent and some older bloke walking towards me.

"You want some?" the older bloke shouted.

I didn't wait. I ran.

"Get the Paki!" Jordan yelled.

I legged it down a side street. They were right behind me. Jordan was faster than his mate, and it was his voice that I could hear. I ran towards a car park that led to the railway bridge. From where I was, it was the fastest way back home.

But, as I reached the bridge, I realised that Jordan was the only one chasing me. At the top of the steps, I stopped. I could see Jordan making for me, but not his mate. As Jordan came up, the older bloke still didn't appear.

"Stuff this!" I said.

I was angry and my heart was pumping like crazy. As Jordan saw me waiting, he stopped and his face changed. The sneer was gone.

"Come on then!" I shouted. "I'm sick of your shit. Let's sort it out!"

I put up my fists. Jordan looked back to the steps.

"No one else is coming," I said. "Just you and me, Jordan."

I stepped towards him.

"You think I'm scared of some dirty Taliban," he said. "I'm EDL hardcore, mate."

But he didn't look very hardcore. And when I thumped him in the mouth, he yelped. I thumped him again and he stumbled, and my brain just exploded.

"COME ON!" I roared.

He was on the floor now, scrambling. I went to hit him again, and he ran. I got hold of his left ankle. But he struggled free and tried to sprint. He didn't see the iron railings until he slammed right into them. Then he disappeared over the side with a scream.

"SHIT!"

I ran to the barrier, praying he hadn't fallen to the tracks below. My head was spinning. I'd wanted to teach him a lesson, not get him killed.

But Jordan hadn't fallen. He was hanging onto a metal strut.

"HELP ME!" he screamed. "PLEASE!"

I thought about going for help, but he'd lose his grip before then. I had to save him. I leaned over the side and jammed my knees against the railings so that I wouldn't fall too.

"Just calm down and hold on!" I told him.

By some miracle, Jordan listened to me and stopped struggling. I managed to get my arms around his chest. I pulled with every bit of strength I had, but he was heavy.

I grabbed his top and tugged at that until he could grab the railings, then I heaved him to safety. We collapsed on the walkway, both of us panting for breath.

When at last I stood up, he just stared at me. It looked like he'd pissed himself.

"Next time, I'll batter you good and proper," I warned.

Jordan didn't say anything.

I left him sitting there and ran home.

12. A BIG DECISION

I didn't tell anyone about what happened with Jordan. I was too scared that he'd go to the police. I kept expecting to be arrested, but that didn't happen.

When Mum told me she'd had an email from Phil to ask if we'd thought about the club's offer, I just shrugged. The Leicester coach had emailed too, but I didn't want to hear that.

"Whatever ..." I said.

Mum wasn't having it. "It is a huge thing to decide," she told me.

"No it's not," I said. "You don't want me to go, so what is there to decide?"

"Of course I don't want you to leave." Mum sighed. "What mother would? But we have to think about you, too."

It was Friday evening and we were getting ready for our busiest night of the week. I'd been doing the potatoes and Mum was preparing spiced chicken for the kebabs.

"What does that mean?" I asked.

"It means that you want to play football, and you've got a great chance to become a pro player," she said. "Your dad and I have spoken about selling the shop and moving with you. If you really want to go, perhaps that is the best option."

You could have knocked me over with a battered haddock. I was that surprised.

"You'd do that?" I asked. "Like, you and Dad would leave everything and come with me?"

Mum nodded. "We can withdraw our offer for the new house and sell the shop. It will take a while, but I don't want you to go alone."

I looked around. The shop was all I'd ever known. When I was a little kid, I'd watched my parents shove sacks of potatoes into the peeling drum and make fresh naan in the electric tandoor oven. I'd sat on the worktop behind the counter and watched them serve up fish and chips, and curry sauce. Like my dad had said – the shop was their life.

"It's only a shop," Mum said. "I'm sure people in Liverpool eat fish and chips too. We could get a nice chippy and you could help out when you weren't training. Your uncle moved to Birmingham, after all."

That was when I remembered Mandip. I'd been so caught up with my own troubles, I hadn't even thought about her and the Brummie Man United fans.

"Mum, did you tell Mandip's parents that we saw her?" I asked.

Mum shook her head. "I'm still deciding what to do," she replied. "Your uncle and aunt are very strict, Baljit. Mandip will be in big trouble if they find out she lied to them."

I thought about how I'd lied to go the first football trial with Danny.

"Can't you just forget that we saw her?" I said. "She wasn't doing anything wrong. You know how hard it is for Asian girls."

"It was worse in my day," Mum told me. "I couldn't even play out with my friends."

"So you understand, then," I said.

"Of course," Mum said. "But how can I lie to your aunt?"

"But you don't have to lie," I pointed out. "You just don't say anything."

"Same difference," Mum told me. "Maybe I should speak to Mandip first ..."

Before I had chance to reply, Dad shouted from the front.

"Bloody customers waiting, innit!" he yelled. "You pair got lost in there?"

I called for Hannah the next evening. When she opened the door, she looked as miserable as I felt.

"You OK?" I asked her.

"Just been thinking," she said. "About you moving away."

She got me some juice and then we sat at the kitchen table.

I smiled, but Hannah didn't smile back.

"You're so lovely, and you make me laugh," she said. "But I don't want a boyfriend who lives a hundred miles away. I want someone I can see all the time."

I stared at her. I didn't know what to say.

"And I don't want to make you feel guilty either," she went on. "I'm just being honest ..."

She sounded like my dad.

"Yeah, I know," I told her.

"So what shall we do?" she asked.

"I haven't accepted the offer yet," I told her.

"But you will, won't you?" Hannah said. "It's your big dream. Your big chance."

I shrugged. For the first time, I started to feel doubt. Did I really want to leave behind everything I knew? Was I really prepared for my parents to sell up and move, just to be close to me?

My phone buzzed in my pocket.

"Hang on," I said. It was a text from Mandip.

Dunno what u said but UR mum is da best! Saved ma LIFE, cuz. Love ya! xxx

I showed Hannah the message.

"So your mum didn't tell Mandip's parents, then?" she asked.

"Guess not," I said.

"She's cool, your mum."

"Yeah," I said. "She's awesome."

★ ★ ★

Later, I lay awake and stared into the darkness. And in my head, I saw Danny with his broken leg. I saw Mum and Dad, watching as someone stuck a "For Sale" sign on the shop. I saw Hannah in her Bob Marley T-shirt, snuggled up against me as we watched rubbish telly together. I could even smell her strawberry shampoo and the perfume she always wore. They were the four most important people in my life. I guess you could say they were my life. Was my dream of playing for Liverpool more important than them? I mean, what use was a dream you couldn't share with the people who meant the most to you?

School broke up for the summer holidays a week later. I'd been thinking and thinking about what I was going to do. In the end, I realised that I already knew. I was just putting it off because it was hard.

School finished at lunchtime, and then I walked Hannah home. When she asked me to come in, I said no.

"Got something important to do," I told her. "Catch you later?"

When I got in, my parents were busy. I sat at my laptop and thought through what I was going to do. However hard it was, I had to do what was best for my future. I found Phil's email address, took a long breath and started to write.

Dear Phil

I've wanted to play for Liverpool FC my whole life. Ever since I first saw the team on Match of the Day, I've dreamed about wearing the red shirt. Coming to meet you all was the best day of my life. I'm honestly so grateful that you asked me to the academy, and that you made me such a great offer. It feels like my wildest dream has come true.

But I've decided I can't move to Liverpool. It's not because I don't want to. It's just that I can't leave my family and friends, and I can't ask my parents to leave everything and move with me. And without the people I care about, it wouldn't mean the same to have my dream come true. I feel awful for turning you down, but I have to. I hope you can forgive me, and that I haven't wasted your time.

I have another offer from Leicester City and I have decided to join them instead. I will continue to play football and I still hope to play for LFC in the future. It has *always been my dream and it always will be.*

This is the hardest decision I've ever had to make. I hope you can understand that it wasn't easy for me. Thank you for giving me such an amazing chance.

Best wishes
Baljit Sandhu

I read through the email about ten times. And then I lay down on my bed and cried.

13. A NEW DREAM

I didn't tell anyone about the email – I was too upset. Instead, I focused on helping out at the shop. I knew I had to tell everyone, but I wanted to wait until I felt OK about it myself.

The next evening, as I served a couple of girls from school, Lacey walked in.

"Mr Sandhu!" she said in her loud voice.

"What you doin' here?" Dad asked. "You not got a shift today."

"I've come to see Baljit." Lacey smiled. "Can I borrow him for a minute?"

Dad told her to wait until the queue was shorter, and then he let me take a break.

"Come outside," Lacey said. "I've got someone who wants to meet you."

When I stepped outside, I saw Jordan Kent. He looked properly sheepish.

"Jordan came to see me," Lacey said. "He said summat about an apology. I'll leave you to it."

As Lacey went back into the chippy, I gulped. I couldn't believe he'd told someone what happened.

"What did you tell her?" I asked.

"Just that I were wrong and you helped me," Jordan said.

I leaned in to whisper in his ear. "I saved your skin, mate. You'd have fallen off the bridge."

Jordan nodded. "I know. I were wrong and I should apologise ..."

"Yeah, but why?" I asked. "Because I saved your life or because you're an ignorant, racist dickhead?"

Jordan's piggy little eyes narrowed.

"Both," he said. "You saved my life and I'm, like, really grateful, mate. Like, seriously."

"What about all that racist crap?" I asked.

"I'm sorry about that too," he said.

Lacey came to the door. "What are you two whispering about?" she asked.

"Nothing," Jordan said. "I were just saying sorry for all the bullying and stuff."

"Too right, you little rat!" Lacey told him. "Like life ain't hard enough for everyone without racists picking on decent people."

"Anyway, I've said me bit," Jordan said. He turned to leave but stopped. "Is it true you're gonna be a Premier League player for Liverpool an' that?" he asked.

"Maybe," I said. I wished people would stop talking about it. "They want me to train with their academy," I told him.

"That's proper mint, that," he said, and walked off.

I watched him leave. I was confused. Like, I was glad he'd apologised. It was a big thing and took guts. But did that mean he would stop being racist? Stop harassing people like me? Or was it just because I'd saved him from falling off the bridge? Lacey broke into my thoughts and told me I should have slapped him.

"Little sewer rat," she added. "Now get me a bag of chips, will you? I'm bloody famished, me."

★ ★ ★

The next morning, Mum asked what I was going to do about Liverpool.

"We need to get things moving," she told me. "The shop won't sell itself and there's so much to think about."

"Er ..." I said. "I've invited Danny and Hannah round for lunch, so can I tell you all then?"

"Tell us what?" Mum asked. "You've made up your mind?"

"Kind of ..."

"Baljit!" she said.

"Mandip told me about what you did," I said. I was keen to change the subject. "That was really cool."

"We had a chat," Mum said with a shrug. "She's a good girl – a lot like me when I was that age. It would have done no good telling her mum.

But I told Mandip she needs to start talking to her parents more."

"They ain't like you and Dad," I told her. "You're not stuck in the Punjab like them – banging on about traditions and that."

"I was born in Leicester," Mum reminded me. "Why would I be stuck in the Punjab?"

"You know what I mean!"

"Well, anyway. It's done now. Me and your dad better start getting the business valued so we can sell it."

"Wait a bit," I said. "It's Sunday. Dad'll still be asleep. Let him chill for a bit."

"You're right," Mum said. "Will you help me make some proper breakfast?"

I nodded. "Go on then."

"And what about this lunch of yours? You should have warned me ..."

"Can't we get pizza or something?" I asked. "Saves you cooking."

"You've thought of everything, haven't you?" Mum smiled.

"That's because you're the best mum in the world," I told her.

When she grabbed me and gave me a big sloppy kiss, I wished I hadn't said anything.

"GERROFF!"

Danny was first. He hopped up the stairs with me behind him, carrying his crutches.

"You OK?" I asked when we got to the top.

"No problem," he said. "Just call me Hoppity McFrog. What's all this about?"

"You'll see," I told him. "There's pizza ..."

"Extra pepperoni, extra cheese?" he asked.

"Of course."

"Well, in that case Hoppity will be staying for lunch."

Hannah turned up ten minutes later. She had a green flowery dress on with big biker boots. As soon as I saw her, I wanted to snog her.

"Hey," she said. "Is this about your decision?"

I nodded. "We've got pizza," I told her.

She tried to smile, but it didn't work and she looked away.

"I just want to know," she said.

Dad was the last one to join us. He'd woken up late and then spent ages in the shower. He had his hair tied in a topknot, but he wasn't wearing a turban. He looked cool.

"Hello, you two," he said to my friends.

"Hey, Mr Sandhu," they replied together.

Dad turned to me. "So what's the big news, innit?" he asked.

I told them all to sit down.

"I've made my mind up about the football," I told them. "And I wanted you all to hear first because you mean the most to me ..."

My mum started to cry at that, and Dad teased her.

"He's going bloody Liverpool, daft woman," he said. "He's not moving to blinking Australia!"

"So you're going?" Hannah said. She tried to keep a smile on her face, but I could tell she was close to tears too.

I thought about the right words to choose.

"I'm going to be playing academy football," I said. "For ... er ..."

I watched Danny look away, and Dad put his hand on Hannah's arm. It made me realise that I had been right.

"For Leicester City – if they still want me."

"Huh?" Danny said.

"What?" Hannah asked.

"Bloody Leicester?" Dad shouted. "But I thought ..."

"I couldn't go," I told him. "I just couldn't. It wouldn't have been fair to make you and Mum move. And I couldn't go because I'd miss Hannah and Danny too much."

"But it's your big dream," Hannah said.

"I'm not giving up," I told her. "I'm just doing it a different way."

"But you love LFC, bro," Danny said.

I felt a lump in my throat. "Yeah," I said. "I do. But I love you lot much more ..."

My mum grabbed me and started to bawl.

"Mum!"

"Bloody hell!" Dad said. "All this drama and you not even going? I'm starving an' all. Where's the blinking pizza, innit?"

As Mum hugged me, Hannah and Danny looked at me with shock. I smiled. It had been really hard, but I was sure I had done the right thing.

"I promised your bloody uncle I'd get him season ticket to Liverpool," Dad said, as he piled his plate high with pizza and chicken wings. "What I gonna say now, innit? Bloody kids – don't know your bottom from your elbow, you ask me."

I grinned at them all, and for the first time in weeks, I felt relaxed. I still had a great chance at playing pro football. And maybe one day I'd end up at LFC. One dream was done, but another one had just started.

14. GAME ON!

About a month later, I started with the Leicester City Academy. It wasn't the same as Liverpool, but I loved it. I even knew two of the other lads.

One afternoon, when I got in from a training session, I saw I had an email from Phil at LFC. He'd been brilliant about what I'd decided, and he had even sent me more LFC goodies in the post. Now, as I ate a couple of bananas and drank a carton of milk, I wondered why he was back in touch.

Hey Baljit (and Mrs Sandhu)

I hope you are well and enjoying your time at Leicester City. I know the coaches at your club very well, and they'll be brilliant for your game. I just wanted to let you know that I will be keeping an eye on you. We take players on at all ages, and maybe you might be ready in two years' time.

For now, remember what you learned about technique, attitude, balance and speed, and enjoy your football. I'll be asking my mates down at Leicester City for progress reports and hope to see you again sometime.

And whatever you do, Baljit, make sure you keep on dreaming.

After everything, LFC were still interested in me. Maybe one day I would end up playing for them. All I had to do was keep working hard, keep improving. Even though I'd just finished training, I grabbed my ball and went out into the garden of our new house. Practice makes perfect, and if I was going to reach my goal, I knew what I had to do. I had everything to play for.

It was Game On!